THE
Berenstain

The Bernstain Bear
Scouts and the Evil
Eye

This book belongs to
MS. JENNIFER DANG

OAY

Look for more books in
The Berenstain Bear Scouts series:

THE Berenstain BEAR SCOUTS
and the
Evil Eye

by Stan & Jan Berenstain
Illustrated by Michael Berenstain

A
LITTLE APPLE
PAPERBACK

SCHOLASTIC INC.
New York Toronto London Auckland Sydney

ISBN 0-590-94488-6

12 11 10 9 8 7 6 5 4 3 2 1   8 9/9 0 1 2 3/0

Printed in the U.S.A.   40

First Scholastic printing, September 1998

• Table of Contents •

and the
Evil Eye

• Chapter 1 •

Favorite and Least Favorite Things

Most of us have favorite things: our favorite color, our favorite TV show, our favorite ice cream flavor. Most of us have least favorite things as well, like too much homework, being grounded, and asparagus. And, of course, the folks in Beartown had their favorite and least favorite things.

The Bear Scouts' favorite thing was earning merit badges. They had a whole slew of them on display in their secret chicken coop clubhouse at the edge of

Farmer Ben's farm. Their least favorite things were crooks and swindlers (although they sort of liked Ralph Ripoff, Beartown's leading crook and swindler).

Ralph Ripoff's favorite thing was cheating folks out of their hard-earned money; his least favorite thing was getting caught at it (and he'd been getting caught at it quite a lot lately).

Gramps's favorite thing was carving monkeys out of peach pits; his least favorite things were Weasel McGreed and his underground gang of henchweasels. Though McGreed and his underground gang had been quiet lately, Gramps wasn't so sure they'd been wiped out by the earthquake that the mighty and powerful Bigpaw had turned back on them.

Bigpaw had his favorite and least favorite things, too. His favorite thing was to sit on his mountain ledge and play on his giant tree-trunk banjo and sing. Bigpaw's

least favorite thing: mosquitoes. That's
right. Mosquitoes.

• Chapter 2 •

Oh, How the Mighty Have Fallen

"Uh-oh," said Scout Brother when he saw Ralph Ripoff setting up his little swindle table right there in the center of town near the police station. Brother and his fellow scouts had come to do some merit-badge research at the library, which was next to the police station.

"He's been warned to stay out of town with those crooked games and tricks of his," said Scout Fred.

"Looks like he's selling something," said Scout Sister.

4

"Let's go see what it is," said Scout Lizzy.

A small crowd had gathered around Ralph. The Bear Scouts joined the crowd. "Four-leaf clovers for sale!" cried Ralph. "Four-leaf clovers for sale! Get your four-leaf covers here! One for a dime! Three for a quarter! Step right up and buy yourself a million dollars' worth of luck for one thin dime!"

Brother stepped right up and said, "Here's a dime, Ralph. I'll take one of those four-leaf clovers."

"What are you doing?" whispered Sister. "You know what a cheat Ralph is!"

"I know exactly what I'm doing," said Brother, holding out his dime.

"Well, if it isn't my favorite cubs, the Bear Scouts," said Ralph. "Here you are! One genuine four-leaf clover, guaranteed to bring you luck. Why don't you get some for your friends? They're three for a quarter, you know. Then you'll have enough for the whole troop."

"No thanks," said Brother. "One will be enough for my purposes."

"What purposes?" asked Sister.

Brother led the troop off to the side and looked closely at the four-leaf clover. "Just as I thought!" he said. "Leave it to Ralph to know how to make a three-leaf clover into a four-leaf clover!"

"A three-leaf clover into a four-leaf clover?" said Fred. "That's impossible."

"Not for Ralph," said Brother. "Here, look." The rest of the troop looked.

"Well, I'll be!" said Sister.

"How about that!" said Fred.

Here's how Ralph made three-leaf clovers into four-leaf clovers:

1. An ordinary three-leaf clover.

2. Split one of the three leaves down the center.

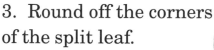

3. Round off the corners of the split leaf.

4. A guaranteed Ralph-style four-leaf clover.

"Ralph better get moving," said Lizzy. "Somebody's going for Chief Bruno."

"Let me have your notebook, Fred," said Brother. Fred handed it to him. Brother opened it to a blank page and wrote a short note. He pushed through the crowd, tore off the note, and handed it to Ralph.

This is what the note said:

"Good grief!" said Ralph. "I must leave you good folks. A personal catastrophe has called me away. My houseboat has broken loose and is roaring down the river."

It was a lie, of course. Lies flowed from Ralph's lips like water from a tap. Ralph did live in a houseboat, but it was stuck in the mud so deep that it would have taken a tugboat to pull it loose.

Ralph folded up his swindle table, stuffed his fake four-leaf clovers into a plastic bag, and made a fast getaway. The scouts followed.

"I want to thank you chaps," said Ralph as the Bear Scouts caught up and fell into step with him.

"Really?" said Brother.

"Absolutely!" said Ralph. "Your timely warning may have saved me considerable inconvenience — perhaps even a night in the hoosegow."

"What about embarrassment?" said

Brother.

"Embarrassment?" said Ralph.

"Yes," said Brother, "the embarrassment of trying to sell those poor, pitiful, fake four-leaf clovers."

"Brother's right. You couldn't fool a fire hydrant with those four-leaf clovers," said Sister as they passed a fire hydrant.

"Or a gumball machine," said Fred as they passed a gumball machine in front of Biff Bruin's Pharmacy.

"Or Grizzly Gus's flannel pajamas," said Lizzy as they passed the Gus place, where Mrs. Gus was hanging out the wash.

They're right, thought Ralph as he looked out over the town. The whole town seemed to be mocking him: the fire hydrants, the gumball machines, the flannel pajamas. Also the houses, stores, and garages. Even the birdies in the trees seemed to be laughing at Ralph's pitiful effort to sell those fake four-leaf clovers.

Ralph slowed to a stop. He sat on the curb. It was as though he were a balloon and suddenly the air had gone out of him. The scouts were taken aback. They weren't used to seeing Ralph in such a condition. They were used to seeing him striding along in his green plaid suit, straw hat, and spats, twirling his cane, always prepared to pick a pocket, cheat an orphan, or rob a widow. It almost seemed as if suddenly the rain had started to fall up, as if fleas had dogs, as if pigs could fly.

Ralph was mumbling something. The scouts moved in close to hear. "It's over," he was saying.

"What's over?" asked Fred.

"My career. I'm finished," said Ralph. "Mighty Ralph Ripoff — winner of the Swindler of the Year Award, king of pickpockets, master of the sleeve card — is down to selling phony four-leaf clovers."

He sighed. "You have no idea how bad it's been. I just seem to have lost my touch. Why, I tried to pick a pocket the other day and all I got for my trouble was a mouse-trap."

"What about that shell game?" asked Brother. "You know, the one where you have three shells and you move 'em around real quick and there's a bean under one of them."

"Ah, yes. The old shell game." He laughed bitterly. "My hand used to be quicker than the eye. But, alas, no more. I was working it the other day. Not only did the sucker pick the right shell, but when I picked it up there was a mouse under it eating the bean." Ralph shook his head. "No, I've got to face it. I've lost my touch. But even worse: *I've lost my confidence.* And when someone in my line of work loses his confidence, then it's time to . . ."

"LOOK FOR A REGULAR JOB!"
shouted the scouts as one.

"A regular job?" said Ralph.

"That's right," said Brother. "A regular, honest job."

"Hmm," said Ralph. "What sort of job?"

"You could be a clerk in a store," said Sister.

"Interesting idea," said Ralph. "I could give the wrong change and pocket the difference."

"Or checkout bear at the supermarket," said Lizzy.

"Uh-huh," said Ralph. "Think of all the coupons I could steal!"

"You could work in the forest with my dad, chopping down trees," said Brother.

"In *these* clothes?" said Ralph, standing up and dusting himself off. Somehow the air had gotten pumped back into Ralph's balloon. "Look, friends, I appreciate your concern. I really do. But I have to look at myself in the mirror every day just as everyone else does, and I don't think I could handle the shame of it."

"The shame of what?" asked Brother.

"The shame of a regular, honest job,"
said Ralph. He reached into his pocket
and took out the plastic bag of fake four-
leaf clovers. "I can let you have the whole
bunch real cheap."

"Ralph," said Sister, "you're impossible."

"I try to be," said Ralph. And off he
went, twirling his cane.

• Chapter 3 •
Soil Scouts

The scouts headed back to the library, where they had some important merit-badge work to do. They had been disappointed when Professor Actual Factual suggested that they try for the Soil Conservation Merit Badge next. "Soil conservation?" they'd complained.

"I know it doesn't sound as exciting as some of the other merit badges you've earned," the professor had said. "But soil conservation is very important. We can't afford to lose it."

"Lose what?" asked Sister.

"The soil," said Actual Factual.

"The soil?" said Sister. "How can we lose the soil? It just lies there."

"Not always," said the professor. "As a matter of fact, we're losing soil every day. It's washing off the riverbanks into the river. We're losing it off the mountain-sides."

"Is that why we're having all those landslides in the mountains?" asked Fred.

"Exactly!" said the professor. "I'm working on the riverbank problem. I'm trying to find out if there are any plants that can hold the soil when the big rains come."

"How is it going so far?" asked Sister.

"It's trial and error — mostly error. But I'm making progress," said the professor. "I plant little patches of different kinds of plants, wait for a big rain, then go see which plants hold their ground." The scouts thought about that for a moment. "I know it doesn't sound very thrilling," he said. "But science isn't all great inventions and wonderful theories. Science is mostly hard work. Trying this, that, and the other until you find something that works."

"We understand, professor, and we'd like to work with you on the river," said Brother.

"Right," said Fred. "I can work on my stone-skipping — I'm up to three skips."

"And we can bring our bathing suits," said Sister.

"And I can touch base with my friends the frogs and the dragonflies," said Lizzy.

"Ah, but you won't be working on the river helping me save the riverbank soil," said the professor. "You'll be working high in the mountains saving mountain soil."

"Oh," said Brother.

"That's right," said Actual Factual. "You'll be doing original research, testing which plants can hold that thin mountain soil in place. It'll be a real challenge.

18

Working in the mountains is difficult at best. It's going to take some real study. The library would be a good place to start. Well, what do you think? Will you do it?"

The scouts huddled for a moment. Then Brother, who often spoke for the scouts, said,

• Chapter 4 •

The Flag Is Up

Ralph had just been putting on a show for the scouts. All that strutting and cane twirling had been a front. As soon as the scouts headed back to the library, the spring went out of his step and the twirl went out of his cane. Even the forest animals knew Ralph wasn't himself as he shuffled along the path to the river. It wasn't until he got close to the riverbank where his houseboat was moored that he quickened his step.

Except that "moored" wasn't exactly the right word. "Stuck" was the right word. The backwater where Ralph kept his houseboat was so filled with soil that had washed from the riverbank that it had turned to mud.

But it wasn't the sight of his stuck-in-the-mud houseboat that caused Ralph to quicken his step. It was the flag on his mailbox. It was in the up position, which meant there was mail in the box. And you never knew with mail. It could mean anything. It could mean that one of his big-time swindler friends needed his help on some scheme to sell gold bricks or fake diamonds. Or it could mean nothing.

In this case, it meant nothing. Because the only thing in his mailbox was this month's copy of *Swindler's Magazine*. Ralph didn't even bother to open it. It would just have the same tired ads for loaded dice, marked cards, and sucker lists of widows and orphans. What Ralph needed wasn't loaded dice, marked cards,

and sucker lists. What Ralph needed was
to regain his confidence! It didn't help that
Squawk, his pet parrot, was welcoming
him home with an unwelcome greeting.

"Get an honest job!" squawked Squawk.
"Get an honest job!"

Ralph had had a long, hard day and wasn't about to take any guff from a parrot. "Why, you little birdbrain," he snarled, and threw his *Swindler's Magazine* at Squawk. The magazine missed, thwacked against the wall, and fell to the floor. It so happened that it fell to the floor open to an article that caught Ralph's attention. *Lost confidence?* said the article in big bold letters. *Try hypnotism!*

"Hypnotism! Of course!" said Ralph. He picked up the magazine and sat in his easy chair. "Who needs shell games and sleeve cards? I'll give them the evil eye! I'll *hypnotize* those suckers out of their money!"

As he began to read, there was a loud *thunk* at the door. He got up and opened it. There was a knife stuck in the door. It pierced a note in a familiar hand. The note said: *There will be a meeting in my office at three o'clock sharp.* It was signed *McGreed.*

Ralph had suspected that Weaselworld had survived the earthquake. Now he was sure. He put the magazine in his pocket and headed for the secret entrance to McGreed's underground empire.

• Chapter 5 •

A Distant Rumble

The library was a big disappointment.
There were lots of books about plants, but
there wasn't a single book about plants
that like to grow on mountainsides. Mrs.
Goodbear, the librarian, tried to help. She
even called the Bear County Library in
Big Bear City. Its card catalog was com-
puterized. But all that got them was a
faster "Sorry, we don't seem to have a
thing on that subject."

"Now what?" asked Sister as they left
the library.

"Beats me," said Brother.

"I'm beginning to see what Actual Factual meant by 'original' research," said Fred.

"We could ask Actual Factual," said Lizzy.

"No," said Brother. "We're going to earn this badge on our own. What we need is a plant expert — somebody who knows all kinds of stuff about plants." Brother stopped in his tracks. "And I know just the expert! We all do!"

"We do?" said Sister.

"Who is it?" asked Fred.

"I'll give you a hint," said Brother. "It's somebody who makes the best chocolate chip cookies in Beartown and is married to a grouchy old guy who carves monkeys out of peach pits."

"Gran, of course!" shouted the rest of the troop. They headed across the town square with Brother in the lead.

Gran really *was* an expert. There were

as many different kinds of plants in Gran's front yard — and her backyard, too — as you'd find in a seed catalog.

As the scouts headed out of town toward Gramps and Gran's, the Great Grizzly Mountains came into view. "Hold it," said Lizzy. "I hear something." Lizzy was so tuned in to nature that she could hear a mosquito burp a hundred yards away. "It's a sort of rumbling sound way off in the mountains," she said.

"Maybe it's one of those landslides the professor is worried about," said Fred.

"Which means," said Brother, "that we'd better get moving with our research." The troop hurried on.

It was a rumbling sound, all right. But it wasn't a landslide. It was Bigpaw doing his favorite thing: singing. Bigpaw was the gigantic throwback to prehistoric cavebears whom Actual Factual and the Bear Scouts had discovered on a fossil hunt. A "living fossil" was what the professor had called him. His rumbling voice was as big as the rest of him, and his singing did sound sort of like a landslide from a distance.

Singing was Bigpaw's favorite thing. He liked nothing better than to sit on his mountain ledge, strum his tree-trunk banjo, and sing. He didn't sing well. But he more than made up in enthusiasm what he lacked in talent. But just when

Bigpaw would get going on his favorite
thing, his least favorite thing would come
and sting him on the nose.

That's why Bigpaw hated mosquitoes.

Bigpaw would try to sing through the mosquito attacks by brushing the insects away. But sometimes he got so angry that he bopped himself on the nose. One time he bopped himself so hard he almost knocked himself off the ledge.

There was nobody there to take note of Bigpaw's strange behavior except the mountain goats, of course. But they had problems of their own finding enough food to eat in the harsh mountain environment. That's the way it is with an environment. If it isn't one thing, it's another. If there wasn't enough soil for plant life, there wouldn't be enough food for animal life, and so on and so forth until there *was* no mountain environment, just a cold, dead mountain range.

That's what's so important about soil conservation. Soil may be just dirt to some folks, but to an environmentalist it's the stuff of life.

• Chapter 6 •

Trouble Ahead

Wow! thought Sister as she looked at the blaze of flowers in Gran's front yard. "Talk about a green thumb!" said Sister to Gran. "You must have two green thumbs and eight green fingers!"

"No, my dear," said Gran with a smile. "It's Mother Nature that has the green thumb. I just try to help her along."

The scouts told Gran about their soil conservation project and how they were looking for plants that would hold their ground in the mountains.

"Hmm," said Gran. "Let me think on it

a bit." As Gran stood there thinking, the scouts looked around for Gramps. He was nowhere to be seen.

"I may be able to help," said Gran. "Come on around back. Now, as I understand it, you're looking for plants that can survive in that harsh mountain environment. While my backyard garden isn't a mountainside, it *is* a hillside. I might just have some plants worth trying on your mountainside."

There was a steep hill leading down into a little valley behind Gramps and Gran's place. It was covered with low-growing plants.

"These plants are mostly different kinds of sedum and ivy," said Gran. "Let me give you some samples to try on your mountainside."

"We'll do the work, Gran," said Brother. "Just show us which plants."

"No, I'd better do it myself," said Gran. "Why don't you go in and talk to Gramps and see if you can coax him out of his foul mood."

"Foul mood?" said Brother.

"What's it about?" asked Sister.

"He's always happy to see you scouts. Just go in and see him. He's in his study," said Gran. Then she headed for her garden shed.

"Who's there?" snarled Gramps when Brother knocked on the study door.

"It's the Bear Scouts, Gramps," said Brother. "May we come in?"

"Sure. Sure," said Gramps.

The scouts could tell he was in a foul mood from the sound of his voice. Gramps, who was very fond of the scouts, was usually eager to show them his newest carving or his latest ship-in-a-bottle project. But not today. He was pacing back and forth with a worried look on his face. You could almost see the black cloud of worry over his head.

"What's the matter, Gramps?" asked Brother.

"There's trouble ahead!" said Gramps.

"What sort of trouble?" asked Sister.

"Weasel trouble," said Gramps. "Nobody as mean, smart, and tough as Weasel McGreed is going to be stopped by a mere earthquake. I don't know where, and I don't know when. But we haven't heard the last of McGreed. Count on it. I can feel it in my bones."

The scouts looked at each other and shrugged. Everybody knew that the weasels had been wiped out in the earthquake. Everybody except Gramps. There was no point in arguing with Gramps's bones. The scouts turned to leave just as Gran appeared at the door.

"I've got a good selection of plants ready," she said. "I've put them in these plastic bags to keep them moist. Each plant has a name tag. There's also a list of some other things you'll need for your project."

"That's great, Gran," said Brother. "Thanks a million!"

Then the scouts headed for their secret clubhouse at the far edge of Farmer Ben's farm. That's where they would organize their expedition.

• Chapter 7 •

The Evil Eye

Ralph was cutting across Farmer Ben's pasture on the way to keeping his date with the archweasel. The idea of using hypnotism to swindle folks out of their money had put the spring back in his step and the dollar signs back in his eyes. He had worked as a hypnotist's assistant back in his carnival days. While the hypnotist dazzled the audience by making some poor sucker bark like a dog, Ralph picked their pockets. So Ralph knew that hypnotism worked and had a general idea how to do it. All he needed was a refresher

course. "Hmm," said Ralph, reading the hypnotism article as he crossed Farmer Ben's cow pasture.

"He's reading some kind of a magazine," said Brother. He was watching Ralph with the field glasses that always hung on a hook in the scouts' secret clubhouse.

"Bad idea!" said Sister.

"Right!" said Fred with a grin. "You should never go across Ben's cow pasture without looking where you're going."

"It's just a matter of seconds till he slips on a cow pie," said Brother. "There he goes!" cried Brother, breaking into laughter.

"Let me have those," said Lizzy, taking the field glasses.

"Let me see!" said Fred, reaching for them.

"Me, too!" demanded Sister.

"Hold it!" said Lizzy, elbowing Fred and Sister aside.

"What is it, Lizzy?" said Brother.

"That magazine Ralph was reading when he slipped," said Lizzy. "I can read it."

Lizzy's fellow scouts didn't doubt that for a second. Lizzy had super eyesight without field glasses. *With* field glasses she could count gnats a mile away.

"What's it say?" said Brother.

"It's about hypnotism," said Lizzy, reading. "'Gain power over others with the evil eye!'"

"The evil eye!" said Sister with a shiver.

"Hypnotism," said Fred, who read the encyclopedia just for fun. "A strange power discovered more than a hundred years ago by that great magician Anton Grizmer."

"Never mind about Grizmer," said Brother. "Ralph Ripoff and hypnotism are a scary combination."

"What can we do about it?" asked Sister.

"Nothing much at the moment," said Brother. "We've got to figure out how we're going to get these plants up the mountain."

Across the pasture, a group of cows watched Ralph pick himself up and brush himself off.

"Blasted cows! Why don't you look where I'm going?" said Ralph. Hmm, he thought. Why don't I try my evil eye on one of these cows?

Being careful to watch his step, he walked over to one of the cows. He took out his watch and swung it gently in front of the calm, quiet, cud-chewing cow. "Look me in the eye, Bossy. Look me deep in the eye. You are coming under my spell. You are coming under my power." The cow followed the movements of the watch as if it were a tennis match.

"Listen very carefully," said Ralph. "You are no longer a cow. You are a bull. An angry, snorting bull."

The cow lowered her head and snorted. She pawed the ground like an angry bull.

"Whoa, Bossy!" said Ralph. He sensed that she was about to charge. And charge she did. She chased Ralph clean across the pasture. Ralph managed to escape over the fence in the nick of time.

• Chapter 8 •

The Beginnings of a Plan

"It worked! It worked!" said Ralph, trying to catch his breath after his long run. Maybe it hadn't been such a good idea making the cow think she was a bull, but that wasn't the point. The point was that there was power in hypnotism. Power over the minds of others. Power over the actions of others. Who needed sleeve cards, loaded dice, and fake four-leaf clovers when he had the power of the evil eye? Of course, there was more to hypnotism than making a sucker bark like a dog or making a cow charge like a bull. He would have to practice. He would have to study.

As he walked along thinking about power over others, he heard a rumbling. At first he thought it was the sound of distant thunder. Then he realized it was the sound of Bigpaw singing way off in the Great Grizzly Mountains. Talk about a tin ear — a *big* tin ear.

Hmm, thought Ralph. Power over others. Power over Bigpaw. Anyone who had power over Bigpaw could . . . what was it McGreed was always saying? "Take over Bear Country, lock, stock, and honeypot." Why not take over Bear Country, lock, stock, honeypot, *and* the folks, fields, forests, factories, and everything else in between? Bigpaw was far and away the strongest force in Bear Country, and anyone who controlled him could control Bear Country. And there were those trouble-making, scheme-foiling Bear Scouts to worry about.

Ralph knew there was one power that hypnotism could not control. At least that's what it said in the magazine. It was the power of love. And Bigpaw loved the Bear Scouts. There was a powerful bond between them. Bigpaw would never do anything to hurt the scouts. But, even so, there was no way of getting close enough to Bigpaw to hypnotize him. The big fellow wasn't too bright, but he was shrewd and wary. One false move in his direction and he could squash you like a grape.

The sound of Bigpaw's singing kept rumbling in Ralph's ear. Hmm, thought Ralph, *the singing*. Yes, maybe the singing . . .

A plan began to form in Ralph's twisted mind. He would need help, of course. But help lay just ahead — in Weaselworld.

• Chapter 9 •
Operation Revenge

Ralph was expected. No sooner had he entered Weaselworld than a troop of armed guards took him in charge and quick-marched him along the rubble-strewn tunnel. The heavy marching was shaking bits of dirt and rocks loose from the damaged tunnel roof. Signs of the earthquake

were everywhere. There were cracked walls, roof props, and blocked-off tunnels. And they were miles from ground zero, where the earthquake had struck.

Ralph was gasping for breath when they finally arrived and the sergeant shouted, "Company, halt!" The troop stopped, but not before a final one-two stomp knocked loose a rock that damaged Ralph's straw hat. "Look what you've done to my hat!" he complained. "This is no way to treat an invited guest. I shall complain to the archweasel himself!"

The sergeant ignored Ralph and pushed him into McGreed's office, where the Big Three were waiting. The Big Three were McGreed; Dr. Boffins, his top scientist; and Stye, his tunnel-tough lieutenant. The room was poorly lit, but Ralph could make out a chair and a large video screen.

"I must protest," said Ralph. "This is no

way to treat a loyal friend. Look at this hat!"

"Siddown and shut up," snarled Stye. Ralph sat down and shut up.

"Listen very carefully, Ralph," said McGreed, his yellow eyes boring in and his needle-sharp teeth glinting. "We have spared no effort to find out who it was that foiled our earthquake scheme. At first we thought it might be those infernal Bear Scouts and perhaps that crazy grandfather of theirs. But that has not turned out to be the case. We believe we have found the culprit. It is a creature whose appearance, habits, and behavior are so strange that we can make no sense of it. But to plan a successful revenge we need to know more about this creature. Dr. Boffins, run the tape!"

The tape was fuzzy and brief and had poor sound. It showed Bigpaw. It showed him stretching, yawning, singing, and

swatting mosquitoes. When the tape stopped, Ralph smiled and said, "That's no creature, that's Bigpaw. And you're right about him foiling your earthquake. When your earthquake surfaced, he simply grabbed a couple of trees, forced the split back together, and sent it back where it came from."

"But that's impossible!" said Dr. Boffins. "That earthquake was a seven on

the Richter scale! There's no way . . ."

"Maybe not," said Ralph. "But it just so happens that I saw him do it with my own eyes."

McGreed and the top brass looked at each other in disbelief.

"As for revenge — forget about it," said Ralph. "I mean, this guy is bigger than a hundred-year-old oak and ten times stronger."

"What about that awful roaring he does?" asked McGreed.

"That's not roaring," said Ralph. "That's singing. Bigpaw loves to sing. That's his favorite thing to do in all the world."

"What about that crazy part where he bashes himself in the nose?"

"Swatting mosquitoes," explained Ralph. "Bigpaw hates mosquitoes. They can't get through his thick fur, but they drive his nose crazy."

"It sounds like you actually know this

guy," said McGreed.

"I know him well," said Ralph, feeling more and more in control. "Which brings me to a little plan I have in mind."

"We're listening," said McGreed.

"As I said, forget about revenge," said Ralph. "Bigpaw could scoop up Weasel-world as if it were an anthill. Besides, why do things the hard way?"

"What's the easy way?" said McGreed.

"It's right here in this magazine." He handed *Swindler's Magazine* to McGreed.

"Hmm," said McGreed. "'Try hypnotism! Gain power over others with the evil eye!' Very interesting." McGreed called for the lights to be turned on and began reading the hypnotism article.

"Who's going to be doing all this hypnotizing?" asked Stye.

"You're looking at him," said Ralph, puffing out his chest.

"You?" snarled Stye. "Since when are

you a hypnotist?"

"Since about twenty minutes ago when I hypnotized one of Farmer Ben's cows. I put her under just like that," said Ralph, snapping his fingers.

"A cow?" said Stye.

"Not to mention the fact that I was a carnival hypnotist years ago," said Ralph, stretching the truth quite a bit.

"Hypnotizing a weak-minded cow is one thing," said Stye. "Let's see you hypnotize me."

"Happy to do so," said Ralph, taking out his watch. "Or, better yet, I'll hypnotize McGreed himself. If that's okay, chief."

"Okay," said McGreed. "Hypnotize away."

Ralph moved close to McGreed. Stye and Dr. Boffins looked on as Ralph began to swing his watch in front of the arch-weasel. "Observe my watch," said Ralph in a low, spooky voice that he remembered

from his carnival days. "Gently
swinging . . . back and forth . . . gently
swinging . . ."

But McGreed wasn't watching the
watch. He was looking into Ralph's eyes.

"Your eyes are getting . . . heavy," said
Ralph.

But it wasn't McGreed's eyes that were
getting heavy.

"You feel . . . you feel a great need to
sleep," said Ralph, his voice getting
weaker and his eyes beginning to close.

McGreed reached out and gently took the watch from Ralph's hand. "Do you hear me, Ralph?" he said. "Do you hear me?"

Ralph nodded his head.

"When you wake up," said McGreed, "you are no longer going to be Ralph. You are going to be Big Red Rooster, king of the barnyard, and it is your job to tell the world the sun has just come up." Then McGreed snapped his fingers and said, "Wake up, Big Red Rooster."

The effect was astounding. As soon as Ralph opened his eyes he began leaping around, flapping his arms, and screaming, *"COCK-A-DOODLE-DOO! COCK-A-DOO-DLE-DOO!"*

"Amazing," said Stye.

"Astonishing," said Dr. Boffins.

McGreed let Ralph be Big Red Rooster for a while. Then he said, "When I snap my fingers, you will once again be Ralph."

He snapped his fingers and Ralph came to.

"Wha-what happened?" said Ralph, looking puzzled.

"Nothing to worry about," said McGreed with a grin. "You and I just had an evil eye contest, and I won. Now, let's get on with Operation Revenge. You mentioned preparations. What sort of preparations did you have in mind?"

COCK-A-DOODLE-DOO!

• Chapter 10 •

Preparations

So it was that while the Bear Scouts were preparing a mountain expedition to conserve soil, Ralph and the archweasel were preparing a mountain expedition to take over Bear Country, lock, stock, and honeypot, and everything in between. The Bear Scouts' preparations included plants, plant food, potting soil, garden tools, and bottles of water, pictures of plant labels for hardy ivy, climbing ivy, creeping sedum, spreading sedum, and sprawling sedum. The Ralph/McGreed expedition included cardboard cutouts of the Bear

Scouts, a portfolio of artwork, a slouch hat, an opera cape, and a giant tongue depressor.

It also happened that the Bear Scouts and the Ralph/McGreed team began climbing the Great Grizzly Mountains at about the same time. The scouts climbed up the mountain on the outside, while the Ralph/McGreed team climbed it from the inside.

McGreed led the way up the twisting, turning, secret passageway that led to a cave near the top of the mountain.

"I wondered how you got that tape of Bigpaw," said Ralph. "He's very wary of strangers."

One of the things the scouts liked about working in the mountains was that it gave them a chance to visit with their great and good friend Bigpaw. Naturally, they chose to start their soil conservation project on Mount Grizzly, where Bigpaw lived. Their plan was to plant the ivy and sedum about halfway up the mountain, then climb the rest of the way to visit Big-paw.

As they climbed they could see what the professor was worried about. The higher they climbed the thinner and patchier the soil became. The scouts were expert climbers (they had long since earned the Rock-climbing Merit Badge).

It was mostly bare rock that they were climbing — bare rock with patches of tired-looking plants hanging on for dear life in the thin, gritty soil.

They rested and snacked when they reached the halfway point. Then they went to work mixing the potting soil into the gritty mountain soil, putting in the plants, watering them with plant food–laced water, patting them down, putting in their little name signs, and hoping for the best when the mountain snow and ice melted and spring rains came.

They couldn't see their friend Bigpaw high up on the ledge in front of his cave. But, about halfway through the job, he began to sing. So they sure could hear him. And since they couldn't get the work done with their fingers in their ears, they had to listen. "Bigpaw has a great voice, but not for singing," said Brother with a grin.

His fellow scouts agreed.

Meanwhile, *inside* the mountain, Ralph and McGreed were still climbing. "Are you sure this is going to work?" snarled McGreed. "Because if it isn't . . ."

"Please, chief, be reasonable," said Ralph. "There's nothing that's sure in life except ticks and fleas."

"Because if it doesn't," continued McGreed, "I'm going to turn you back into Big Red Rooster faster than you can say 'Cock-a-doodle-do!' And that's just for starters!"

That's when they heard it: Bigpaw's singing echoing down through the passageway. McGreed gritted his teeth and put his fingers in his ears.

"No, chief! No!" pleaded Ralph. "No gritting! No fingers in the ears! Just wild applause and shouts of 'Bravo! Bravo!' Try to remember, we *love* Bigpaw's singing. That's why we've come. That's why I've brought Dr. McGreed, the great singing expert, to hear his wonderful voice."

"Just remember, you pea-brained idiot," snarled McGreed. "If this scheme of yours doesn't work . . ."

But there was no time for talking. They had reached the secret cave that opened onto Bigpaw's mountain. It was time for action.

• Chapter 11 •

Why You Come See Bigpaw?

"Bravo! Bravo!" shouted Ralph as he and McGreed came out of the cave into the clear mountain air.

And there he was, the great creature himself, strumming his tree-trunk banjo and singing his heart out.

"Applaud! Shout 'Bravo!'" whispered Ralph to McGreed. McGreed applauded and shouted, "Bravo!"

Bigpaw stopped singing the instant he saw Ralph and the funny little fellow in the opera cape and slouch hat. "You Ralph Ripoff," said Bigpaw, glowering down at his visitors. "You bad guy. You try hurt my little Bear Scout friends!" He moved toward the visitors, holding the banjo in the club position.

"Hurt the Bear Scouts?" protested Ralph. "You do me an injustice, sir! I love the Bear Scouts. They are my dearest little friends! They are as dear to me as my own blood nieces and nephews. Why, I love

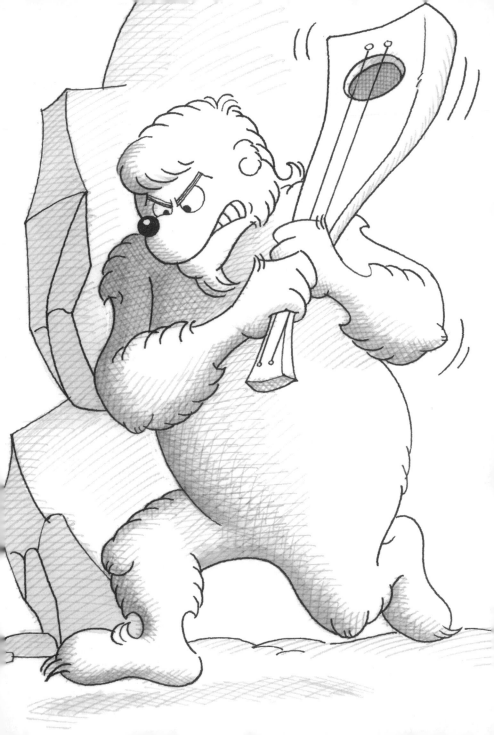

the Bear Scouts so much I carry their pictures with me always!" Ralph turned to McGreed. "Quick, chief, show 'em the cutouts!" McGreed set the Bear Scout cutouts up on the ledge.

Bigpaw stopped glowering and lowered his banjo. "Why you here? Why you come see Bigpaw?"

"Why we here?" said Ralph. "Why we come see Bigpaw? Surely you jest. We've come to hear Bigpaw sing, of course."

Bigpaw thought about that for a moment. "Bigpaw love to sing," he said.

"Certainly you love to sing. Why *wouldn't* you love to sing with such a thrilling, wonderful voice as yours?"

"Bigpaw love to sing," repeated the big fellow.

"And why else would I have brought the great Dr. McGreed with me?" said Ralph.

"Bigpaw not sick," said the giant.

"Not that sort of doctor, my good fellow,"

said Ralph. "Dr. McGreed is a doctor of singing. He is, in fact, the world's greatest expert on the art of vibrato. He is a student of the uvula — that little thing that dangles at the back of your throat. And, amazing as it may seem, the good doctor wishes to take you under his wing."

"Singing doctor got no wings," said Bigpaw, raising his banjo back to the club position.

"You misunderstand!" said Ralph. "'Under his wing' is just an expression — a manner of speaking, as it were." Bigpaw resumed full glower. "What it really means is that the good doctor wishes you to be his protégé."

"Bigpaw think you try to fool him with big words," said the singing giant.

"For pete's sake, take over, chief!" whispered Ralph to McGreed. "I'm running out of steam. And it's now or never. I don't think he's buying our act."

McGreed took his courage in his hands, stepped forward, and said, "I am zee great opera expert, and you are wasting zee time. Do you wish to sing in zee opera or not?"

"Opra?" said Bigpaw. "What opra?"

"What's opera? What's opera?" cried McGreed, swirling his cape and jabbing the air with his ivory-headed walking stick. "Opera is zee greatest singing! To sing zee operas of Beartoveen, Bearzart, and Bearcini is to reach zee sublime." Bigpaw seemed interested.

"And look here, big fellow," said Ralph, opening the portfolio. "Here are pictures of how you'll look in the different operas. Here you are in *William Tell* — you know, the bear who had to shoot the apple off his cub's head. And here you are singing *Falstaff,* the big fat guy who gets all the laughs."

"Bigpaw like pictures!" said Bigpaw. "Bigpaw look nice singing opra. How I get to sing opra?"

"Nothing could be simpler, my dear fellow," said Ralph. "As soon as the good doctor examines your uvula, we'll start booking the concert tour."

"What's that?" asked Bigpaw.

"You know, that little thing in your throat," said Ralph. "It will allow Dr. McGreed to decide which operas will be best for you. Now, if you just help the doctor look in your throat."

Bigpaw was all for it. "Bigpaw go on concert tour! Goody!" He reached down and, using his Dumpster-size paw as an elevator, lifted the good doctor and his giant tongue depressor up ten stories.

• Chapter 12 •

Familiar Voices!

"What in the world do you suppose is going on?" said Sister.

The scouts were watching from behind
some rocks. They had finished their work
and climbed the rest of the way to visit
Bigpaw. But as they got near Bigpaw's
ledge, they heard voices. *Familiar* voices.
The voices of Ralph Ripoff and the archweasel McGreed.

"I haven't a clue as to what's going on,"
said Brother. "But whatever it is, it's not
good."

"Open your mouth and say, 'Ah,'" or-

dered McGreed. Bigpaw did as ordered. Of course, McGreed's real purpose was to get in position to hypnotize the giant. Once he gained power over the strongest force in Bear Country, control of all Bear Country would be within easy reach.

McGreed didn't bother with a watch. He just climbed over Bigpaw's swollen, mosquito-bitten nose and zapped him with the evil eye. "Listen to the voice of your master, Bigpaw," said McGreed.

"Bigpaw listen," said Bigpaw, in a sleepy voice.

"Your eyelids are getting heavy," said McGreed, staring into Bigpaw's eyes.

"Eyelids getting heavy," said Bigpaw.

"You feel a deep, deep sleep coming on. . . ."

That's when the Bear Scouts caught on to what was happening. "Good grief!" cried Brother. "He's hypnotizing Bigpaw!"

"Of course!" said Lizzy. "That's what Ralph must have been reading about in *Swindler's Magazine!*"

"Hmm," said Brother. "If Ralph and hypnotism were a dangerous combination, Ralph, McGreed, and hypnotism are a hundred times as dangerous."

"That's right," said Fred. "If McGreed gets Bigpaw under his control, he could control all of Bear Country in a matter of days!"

"We've got to do something!" cried Lizzy.

"But what?" cried Sister.

McGreed had put Bigpaw into a deep sleep. "When you wake up," said McGreed, "you will be my servant, and I will be your master. You will obey my every command, whatever it may be."

"Yes, master," said Bigpaw.

"When I snap my fingers," said McGreed, "you will wake up and put me down."

McGreed snapped his fingers. Bigpaw woke up and put McGreed down.

"Bigpaw," said McGreed. "Who am I?"

"You my master," said Bigpaw.

"And who are you?" said McGreed.

"I your servant," said Bigpaw.

"Do the thing with the Bear Scouts, chief," urged Ralph. He set up the cardboard Bear Scout cutouts on the ledge.

"Your nose is swollen," said McGreed. "Why is that?"

"Mosquitoes bite Bigpaw's nose," said the big fellow. "Bigpaw hate mosquitoes,"

he said, looking around for some. "Where mosquitoes? Bigpaw bash 'em!"

"They're right there," said McGreed, pointing to the Bear Scout cutouts.

They were very good cutouts. They looked exactly like the Bear Scouts. But to the deeply hypnotized Bigpaw they looked exactly like mosquitoes. "Bigpaw hate mosquitoes!" he roared. "Bigpaw bash 'em!" He rushed at the Bear Scout cutouts and beat them to a pulp.

"Stop! Stop!" cried the scouts as they poured out from behind the rocks. "Those are bad guys! Don't listen to them! Don't listen to them!"

"It's those infernal Bear Scouts," snarled McGreed. "They foiled our last scheme. It's time to put an end to them! Bigpaw, deal with those mosquitoes!"

Bigpaw looked at the scouts. "Bigpaw hate mosquitoes. Mosquitoes bite Bigpaw's nose. Make it itch. Make it sore." He moved toward the Bear Scouts, swinging his clublike banjo. But it seemed to Ralph that the big guy's heart wasn't really in it. Ralph began to worry a bit. What was it that the magazine had said about the power of hypnotism?

McGreed urged Bigpaw on. "Bash 'em! Smash 'em!" he shouted. "Give those rotten mosquitoes what for!"

Bigpaw was about to do just that. He had backed the scouts up against the mountain and was about to smash them with his mighty banjo. The scouts realized that their friend was hypnotized and didn't know what he was doing. "Don't, Bigpaw! Don't!" they screamed. "We're not mosquitoes! We're the Bear Scouts! We're your friends! We love each other!"

That was what Ralph was trying to re-member from the magazine: that there was one power hypnotism couldn't over-come — the power of love!

And so it was that Bigpaw did not smash the Bear Scouts. Because what it said in the magazine was true. Just as Bigpaw was about to strike, the power of love broke through. Bigpaw looked at the scouts as if for the first time. "You not mosquitoes," he said. "You Bear Scouts. You my friends."

"I think we'd better get out of here fast," said Ralph. He and McGreed began to edge toward the getaway cave.

Bigpaw turned to Ralph and McGreed. "You not Bigpaw's friends!" he said, raising his banjo. "You bad guys! Bigpaw not hurt Bear Scouts. Bigpaw hurt bad guys!" With that, Bigpaw charged.

"Run for your life!" screamed Ralph. The miserable, scheming twosome streaked for the cave. They got there a split second before Bigpaw hit the cave entrance so hard that the mountain shook and the cave collapsed. There was a rumble inside the mountain.

"Those guys never bother Bigpaw again," said the big fellow.

Brother put his ear to the mountain. "Those guys will never bother *anybody* again," he said.

Bigpaw knelt down and held up his great palm. "Way to go!" said Brother as one by one the Bear Scouts stepped up and high-fived their enormous friend.

• Chapter 13 •

Big Barking Dog

It was too much to say that Ralph and McGreed would never bother anyone again. It *was* fair to say that the collapse of the cave and the rockslide that followed would put them out of action for quite a

while. The rockslide followed Ralph and the great singing expert all the way back down the secret, twisting, turning passageway and dumped them, tattered and torn, in Weaselworld. Ralph crawled out of

the rock pile before McGreed came to and made a fast getaway. He certainly wasn't going to hang around and let McGreed turn him back into Big Red Rooster.

As Ralph made his way back to his houseboat, he thought about hypnotism and the events of the day. Operation Revenge was perhaps just too much of a good thing. But that didn't mean hypnotism couldn't be a useful tool in separating folks from their money. He would need more practice, that's all.

Ralph was exhausted when he got back to his houseboat. He dragged himself up the gangplank and collapsed in his easy chair. Once again, Squawk, his pet parrot, greeted him with an unwelcome greeting. "Get a regular job! Get a regular job!" squawked Squawk.

Hmm, more practice, thought Ralph, as he stared at the parrot. He walked over to the parrot, took out his watch, and started swinging it.

"You are getting sleepy," said Ralph.

"You are getting sleepy," repeated Squawk.

"When I say the words 'evil eye' you will no longer be yourself," said Ralph.

"When I say the words 'evil eye' you will no longer be yourself," repeated Squawk.

"You will be Big Barking Dog," said Ralph.

"You will be Big Barking Dog," repeated Squawk.

"And so I say *evil eye!*" cried Ralph.

No sooner had Squawk repeated the words "evil eye" than Ralph began running around on all fours barking and chewing the furniture. That's what he was doing when the scouts arrived. The scouts had come to see if Ralph had survived.

"Arf! Arf!" barked Ralph, taking a bite out of the easy chair.

"What do you suppose happened?" said Fred.

"It looks to me like Ralph tried to hypnotize Squawk and it backfired," said Sister.

"Ralph," said Brother. "When I snap my fingers, you will once again be your old rotten self." Brother snapped his fingers,

and once again Ralph was his old rotten self.

"Hi, guys," said Ralph. "What's happening?"

The scouts looked at him as if he were some strange creature from a distant planet. "Later," said Brother as he and the scouts exited the houseboat and headed for their clubhouse.

The scouts earned their Soil Conservation Merit Badge, and they were very proud of it. But they were just as proud of the fact that they had saved Bear Country from the evil influence of . . .
THE EVIL EYE!

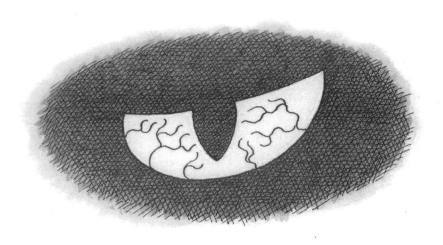

• About the Authors •

Stan and Jan Berenstain have been writing and illustrating books about bears for more than thirty years. Their very first book about the Bear Scout characters was published in 1967. Through the years the Bear Scouts have done their best to defend the weak, catch the crooked, joust against the unjust, and rally against rottenness of all kinds. In fact, the scouts have done such a great job of living up to the Bear Scout Oath, the authors say, that "they deserve a series of their own."

Stan and Jan Berenstain live in Bucks County, Pennsylvania. They have two sons, Michael and Leo, and four grandchildren. Michael is an artist, and Leo is a writer. Michael did the pictures in this book.

Don't Miss

THE *Berenstain* **BEAR SCOUTS**

and the Rip-off Queen

The scouts followed Ms. Goodbear to the legal section, where they checked the return shelves. On one of them rested a thick leather-bound volume titled *Laws of Grizzly River County. Volume I: Beartown, Bearville, and Bruinville Districts.*

"Yes," said Ms. Goodbear. "This is the one Ralph looked through. Now, if you'll excuse me, I must get back to the front desk. Good luck."

The scouts carried the heavy volume to a nearby table and began to read. They had barely gotten through five pages of dense legal language when Sister shook her head. "This is a wild goose chase," she said. "There must be four hundred pages on Beartown in this book. How are we going to figure out what Ralph was looking for?"

But just then Fred turned a page and cried, "Aha!"

"Shhh," said Lizzy. "This is a library, remember?"

"*Aha,*" Fred whispered. "Here's a page corner that's been turned down. I'll bet Ralph did that so he could find this page again after going through the rest of the Beartown stuff. Let's see if there are any other corners turned down."

There weren't. Fred turned back to the one he'd found. "Hmm," he said. "It's about the gambling laws. It says that at one time gambling was outlawed only within the city limits of Beartown, but now it's illegal in the entire district. Then it says to see Appendix IV for a map showing the city and district boundaries."

"Gambling?" said Sister. "That sure sounds like Ralph."

"Hmm," said Fred. "*Gambling. Riverboat . . .*" Suddenly his eyes lit up. "Of course! *Riverboat gambling!* Ralph wants to turn his houseboat into a riverboat gambling business!"

"Yeah!" said Sister. "And when he found out that gambling is outlawed in the entire district he decided to bribe Mayor Honeypot to look the other way!"

"Just wait till we tell the mayor-for-a-day about this!" said Lizzy. "He can break this case wide open to the Press Club this afternoon!"

THE *Berenstain* BEAR® SCOUTS
by Stan & Jan Berenstain

Join Scouts Brother, Sister, Fred, and Lizzy as they defend the weak, catch the crooked, joust against the unjust, and rally against rottenness of all kinds!

❏ BBF60384-1	The Berenstain Bear Scouts and the Coughing Catfish	$2.99
❏ BBF60380-9	The Berenstain Bear Scouts and the Humongous Pumpkin	$2.99
❏ BBF60385-X	The Berenstain Bear Scouts and the Sci-Fi Pizza	$2.99
❏ BBF94473-8	The Berenstain Bear Scouts and the Sinister Smoke Ring	$3.50
❏ BBF60383-3	The Berenstain Bear Scouts and the Terrible Talking Termite	$2.99
❏ BBF60386-8	The Berenstain Bear Scouts Ghost Versus Ghost	$2.99
❏ BBF60379-5	The Berenstain Bear Scouts in Giant Bat Cave	$2.99
❏ BBF60381-7	The Berenstain Bear Scouts Meet Bigpaw	$2.99
❏ BBF60382-5	The Berenstain Bear Scouts Save That Backscratcher	$2.99
❏ BBF94475-4	The Berenstain Bear Scouts and the Magic Crystal Caper	$3.50
❏ BBF94477-0	The Berenstain Bear Scouts and the Run-Amuck Robot	$3.50
❏ BBF94479-7	The Berenstain Bear Scouts and the Ice Monster	$3.50
❏ BBF94481-9	The Berenstain Bear Scouts and the Really Big Disaster	$3.50

© 1997 Berenstain Enterprises, Inc.

Available wherever you buy books or use this order form.

Send orders to:
Scholastic Inc., P.O. Box 7502, Jefferson City, MO 65102-7502

Please send me the books I have checked above. I am enclosing $_____(please add $2.00 to cover shipping and handling). Send check or money order — no cash or C.O.D.s please.

Name_____ Birthdate ____/____/____
M   D   Y

Address_____

City_____ State _____ Zip_____

BBSE897